Mary-Ellen O'Keefe's Word-

Written by Tom E. Neely

Illustrated by Sharad Kumar

Cover Design and Interior Layout by Tom E. Neely

Copyright © 2014

Tom E. Neely

All Rights Reserved

ISBN-13: 978-1502444257

ISBN-10: 1502444259

For Angelina, Luke, and Sophia

In the quiet little town of Winchester-Bofeef
Lived a not-so-quiet kid named Mary-Ellen O'Kcefe.

Mary-Ellen loved to talk. She loved to sing, even **SCREAM!**
She was not exactly shy (if you know what I mean).

You could ask that kid anything, and she would *always* retort.
Mary-Ellen treated talking like it was some kind of sport!

She loved to chat with her sister, whose name was Deanna.
They played "Dress-Up", sang songs, and ate tons of bananas!

She shouted out colors, and letters, and more!
She told goofy stories. She could count to ninety-four!

She made up funny rhymes. She could twiddle her thumbs.
Mary-Ellen told jokes while she banged on her drums!

You see, her voice was her instrument and she used it to SHOUT!
And all the words in her head used her mouth to come out!

When Mary-Ellen was home, she was brave! She was cool!
Then one day Mom said, "It's time for you to start school."

Mary-Ellen was excited! She couldn't wait to begin!
But on the way to school that first day, it began to sink in...

"School will be different," she thought, "Different and weird."
"I won't know anyone there... I might get scared!"

But she pushed all those scary thoughts out of her mind.
Then she took a deep breath and with Mom right behind,

She walked into that school, (but it sure wasn't easy).
And as Mom walked away, Mary-Ellen felt queasy...

School was different and new - but it wasn't too scary.
There were other kids there with names like Jill, Lou, and Harry.

Still, Mary-Ellen felt odd on that very first day.
And for the first time ever, she had **nothing** to say!

It felt like her tongue was tied up in a knot.
All the other kids talked but Mary-Ellen <u>did not</u>!

School wasn't like home and that made her shy.
She just did not feel like talking, but she wasn't sure why.

When she first met her teacher, Miss Lulu-Gaboore,
Mary-Ellen said nothing! She just looked down at the floor!

You see, she wanted to say all the things she could do,
But it felt like her mouth was stuck shut with some glue!

This is strange! It's not normal! Mary-Ellen's never quiet!
It was like she was on some sort of *Word-Speaking Diet!*

Then finally, it was time to go home for the day.
She gave Mom a BIG HUG and they went on their way.

And as soon as Mary-Ellen climbed into that van,
Words came out of her mouth just like worms from a can!

She couldn't be silenced! She just wouldn't clam up!
She said so many things, Mom could hardly keep up!

She talked all the way home! She yapped all ride long.
(So naturally, Mom thought that nothing was wrong.)

And once they got home, she made even more noise.
She talked to her dolls! She talked to her toys!

She told stories during dinner, and in the bathtub, too.
She told her whole family all the things that she knew!

Then she *finally* stopped talking once she climbed into bed,
And she carefully tucked-in the words in her head.

She fell asleep quickly. She was all tuckered out.
(She slept with her mouth shut so no words would fall out!)

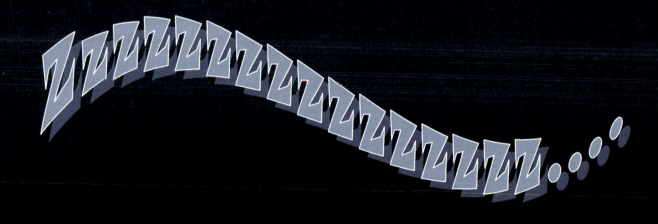

And the next day started just as the last day had ended,
Mary-Ellen woke up talking! She left no car un-bended!

She said "Good Morning, Mister Pillow! Wake Up, Mister Bear!"
And then she talked the whole time Mom was combing her hair!

And when it was time to get ready for school,
She ran down to eat breakfast and climbed up on her stool...

And as you probably guessed, she talked while she ate!
(Until there were nothing but crumbs on her plate.)

Then she talked to those crumbs! She gave each one a name!
And Deanna just LOVED that crazy Crumb-Naming Game!

Then they drove off to school - it was time for Day Two.
Mary-Ellen felt nervous again as school came into view...

She walked into school slowly and she hung up her coat.
Then it happened again! Her words got stuck in her throat!

When Miss Lulu-Gaboore said "Hello! How are you?"
Mary-Ellen said nothing! She just stared down at her shoe!

This is strange! It's not normal! Mary-Ellen's not quiet!
It was like she was <u>back</u> on that *Word-Speaking Diet!*

Mom noticed too, and thought "This isn't funny..."
"What's wrong, Mary-Ellen? Use your words, Honey."

But the words wouldn't come. Not a "Fine" or a "Good"
Mary-Ellen just stood there - like a shy person would!

When the teacher asked questions whose answers she knew,
Mary-Ellen just sat there. She hardly said "Boo!"

And because she was quiet, no one knew she was gabby.
(Some kids in her class even thought she was crabby!)

And this went on for weeks - round after round.
At home she was chatty, but at school - *not a sound.*

This "Shy-Acting Act" was starting to get in the way,
Because we all know how much Mary-Ellen O'Keefe has to say!

So one afternoon, Mom looked her right in the eye,
And tried to explain to Mary-Ellen why she shouldn't be shy:

"You've got to speak up! You can't keep your words hid!
Or how will anyone learn that you're such a great kid?

If you don't use your words no one ever will know,
That at home you play drums and you put on great shows!

And no one ever will hear of your Crumb-Naming Game!
Or how you jump on your bed, and that you spell your own name!

I promise you, Kiddo - you'll knock off their socks!
If you'll just let them see that you're a real chatterbox!

I know you can do it, but it must be YOUR CHOICE,
To open your mouth and let THE WORLD hear your voice!"

What Mom said made sense, and Mary-Ellen knew it.

Mary-Ellen had to change, and it was up to her to do it!

So...

The next morning she decided (at exactly 7:44),
That Mary-Ellen O'Keefe would not be shy anymore!

She marched into that class and she hung up her jacket
But instead of being quiet...she made a **HUGE RACKET!**

She said "Hello, Nice to see you!" to Miss Lulu-Gaboore
(Who, by the way, was so shocked she nearly fell to floor!)

She said "Hello!" to each student and called each kid by name!
Then she taught that whole class her famous Crumb-Naming Game!

This was easy she thought, and a whole lot more fun,
Than sitting in silence and biting her tongue!

Speaking up was fantastic (once she finally tried it).
It was so much more fun than that *Word-Speaking Diet!*

And from that day forward, she never, ever looked back.
And she never again put on that "Shy-Acting Act!"

And for the rest of the year she did so much voice-raising,
That her classmates all said,

"She's not shy - she's AMAZING!"

The End

11196557R00024

Made in the USA
Monee, IL
07 September 2019